Khushiyon Ki Chaabi

Flairs and Glairs

Publication House

"Khushiyon Ki Chaabi"

ISBN No: " 9789390799787"
1st Edition
Language – English and Hindi

Flairs and Glairs
Publication House
Regd. Under MSME Act.

Disclaimer

This is a work of fiction and solely represent the thoughts of the corresponding authors of the articles. Our editors have tried their best to edit the content of all the authors and check the plagiarism.

All the write-ups in this book are unique and are only published in this book.

In case any plagiarism or error is found, only the author is responsible alone, and not the publisher or the Compilers.

Cover Designing and Book Formatting
Shubham Shah and Ishani Agarwal

Co Authors

1) Shubham Shah (Founder)
2) Ishani Agarwal (Co-Founder And Compiler)
3) Anjana Agarwal
4) Ishika Agarwal
5) Amina Sheikh
6) Debanjana Ghatak
7) Divya Baghel
8) Dr B Farheen Khan
9) G B Akshaya
10) Grishma Ninave
11) Kohinur Ali Khan
12) Mahwash Ali
13) Manjuladevi Vs
14) Meetu Chopra
15) Monica Baradia
16) Ms Ishrat Jahan Noormohammed Khan
17) Neha Rahi
18) Payal Purushottam Indani
19) Prachi Mayuresh Kunkalienkar
20) Pratik Premraj Bhala
21) Rabadiya Gopi D
22) Sakshi Maheshwari
23) Tejeshwar Pandey
24) Zala Ramiben Devasibhai Sandeshi

Shubham Shah

(Founder- Flairs and Glairs)

Shubham Shah, an entrepreneur at "Flairs & Glairs" a brand with dynamics in events organizing and cultural educational pan INDIA, is a 26yrs old guy who recently has entered the digital platform of imprinting emotions. He has initiated with his own open mic platform to help budding poets and aspiring writers under his brand named as "Teekhe Zasbaaat"
He is a commerce graduate from the Bhagalpur City of Bihar. He states Writing has impersonated him since childhood and he has now been writing for over a decade!

Cooking, on the other hand, is his passion! He also mentions, trying out new things just tickles him!

When asked sir, Why SPICY EMOTIONS?

He smiled and added, "agar jasbaat teekhe na ho toh wo jasbaat kahan" Spices are all that blends! So do his words!

As a chef, he presents to you his dish! Hot and freshly served! Taste it! Feel it! Enjoy it! You can also find his writing in the Book "Teekhe Zasbaaat" and 50+ Co-authored anthologies. With his passion to explore opportunities across Platforms, he is working with keen devotion and We wish him all the very best for his future ventures.

He is Featured in the International Magazine DeMode for his upcoming solo novel.

He is Approved by Ne8x for its Lit Fest, and is a Golden Star Awards 2020 Winner.

He is a India Book of Records Holder for his Anthology Satrang, and has the Grandmaster title by Asia Book of Records, for the same.

He has also been featured in Prabhat Khabar, Dainik Jagran, and a lot of other Newspapers in Bihar for his achievements.

He has been a proud co-author to

India Book Of Records (Title- Black)

World Book Of Records (Title -15 Wonders of Poetries)

India Book Of Records (Title - Aaina)

Vajra World Records Holder (Title - Gustakhi Maaf Hai)

High Range of Records Holder (Title - Gustakhi Maaf Hai)

Indian Book of Records

(Title - Road from Worst to Best)

Share your reviews on his

INSTAGRAM

@spicy_emotions
@shubham4shah

Or via email on

shubham2shah@gmail.com

To stay tuned to his work and opportunities follow his business Handles

INSTAGRAM   FACEBOOK   YOUTUBE

@flairsandglairs
@teekhezasbaaat

WEBSITE:

https://flairsandglairs.in/
https://flairsandglairs.com/

Khushiyaan

Paas aai jo Khushiyaan wo Azeez hai
Kyuki Tu Mere Kareeb hai

Muskuraane Laga Hu…
Kyuki Goonj rahi teri hasi hai

Paas aao thoda payal ki jhankaar sunao
Mai Pareshan hu, Suno na thodi raahat pahuchao

Ishani Agarwal (CoFounder) (compiler)

Ishani Agarwal hails from the City of Joy, Kolkata. She is the co-founder of her Community "Teekhe Zasbaaat" and Flairs and Glairs Publication.

Been a Compiler for 45+ Anthologies, she is in the process for more. Co-authored in 150+ Anthologies. She is a India Book of Records Holder, a Vajra World Records Holder, a High Range of Records Holder, an OMG Book of Records Holder and a Bravo Record holder.

Approved by Ne8x for its Lit Fest 2020, and Literary Icon 2020. Also a Golden Star Awards Winner 2020.

She has also been awarded with India Star Republic Award 2021, a part of She Awards by Awards Arc and Winner of Nari Samman 2021 by Literoma.

She is also selected as Best Achiever of the Year by AwardsArc and Most Challenging Compiler Award by Spectrum Awards.

She has been featured by the National Magazine "Taree Zameen Par" with the title 'unstoppable'.

Also featured in the International Magazine DeMode for her upcoming solo novel, she is proud to write on social issues, and is happy with the love she is receiving.

Connect with her on Instagram: @Ishani_agarwal_quotes / @compilations_so_far

The Story Of Those Kids

The families were very close. They stayed in the same complex since a very long time. Their kids had been friends since childhood.

Their day would start and end together. They were in the same school, same class. They ate together, studied together. They were inseparable.

However, by the time they grew up, their priorities changed. Riya turned out to be a snob. Studied in a rich school, she got used to boys surrounding her all the time in their expensive cars, giving her expensive gifts, and spending lavishly on her. She forgot her childhood love.

Byt Noyel on the other hand had loved Riya from the beginning. For him, she was the only one. Suffering from a financial crunch, he studied in a mediocre school. With a very good upbringing, Noyel turned out to be a doctor. Whenever he would go express his emotions to Riya, she would shoo him away.

There were enough females behind Noyel too by now, for he was a handsome man.

It was only at the time of need, that Riya would Remember Noyel, and like a fool, he would always help her.

Time went on, and Noyel gave up on pursuing Riya. He finally decided to settle down.

It was at that time, that Riya had started realising Noyel's worth. When other guys would shout at her for small mistakes, she would think about how Noyel would explain her things patiently.

While other guys wanted her only for her body, Noyel had always loved her soul. Just the day when she decided to express her feelings to Noyel, she got to know he was ready to see another girl. She was dejected and heartbroken.

Her parents saw her that way, and informed Noyel's parents on the same. When Noyel got to know about it, he was in the seventh sky.
He was overjoyed.

But he wanted Riya to suffer a bit.
So they made a plan.
They arranged for a fake ring ceremony for Noyel. They informed Riya about it 2 days before the main day. Her parents saw her cry for 2 days. Noyel personally invited Riya to attend the event, so she could not say no
On the day of the event, Riya got ready, and went to the venue. It was quiet there.
But when she saw Noyel decked up as the Groom, she couldn't control her tears.
With tears, she went up ahead to Noyel, and told him her feelings.
On listening, Noyel started laughing.
He then gave her a beautiful lehenga, and asked her to get dressed. She couldn't understand what was happening.
It was then, that Noyel told her it was their engagement today. And without the Bride, an engagement was not possible.

Riya couldn't control her happiness. She was so happy.
In the end, she found her Love. Her true love. Someone, who was genuine with her. Someone, who did not want to change her.
What changed, was Riya's life. It changed for the best.
Since then on, there was a constant smile on Riya's face. Noyel made sure of that.

The Short-Lived Happiness

She wanted to start her day by witnessing the beauty of the Sun Rising. However, her happiness was Clogged by something, she could never imagine.
For, her waking up early is what led to her rape in the first place, and filled her life with Darkness.

Happiness Is What Mattered

The kids were varied.
Small and big,
Young and old,
Black and white,
Thin and fat.
They had never expected to find so much happiness at one place.
Though they belonged to different caste and culture,
The environment of that orphanage was diverse enough to make the childless couple happy.

They couldn't care more of the color or caste of the kid,
But they enjoyed being around those little ones.
It was true happiness in the best sense.

Anjana Agarwal

I am Anjana Agarwal.
Writing has been my way of expression since i was small. Itz coz writing gives me happiness.
Born n brought up in Shelling, married in Kolkata, its through words that i portray emotions best.
Been a Co-author in 50+ Anthologies in the past 1 yr.
Insta handle: anjana5408

Ishika Agarwal

Ishika Agarwal.
Being a class 12 student, my imagination ran wild. I tried penning down my imaginations.
Love Writing. It is nothing else but a passion.
From Kolkata.
Also, into extracurricular activities!
Appreciated by India Book of Records for my solo Book, "Love – A gift or a curse".
Been a Co-author in 70+ anthologies in the recent past.
Insta handle: ishika_agarwal13

Amina Sheikh

She is a student..
She started her first anthology on Captured in your eyes book
and many more anthology books..   And soon started her
journey with falirs n glairs..
She about writing...
She like to write on love, emotions, and inspirational quotes..If
you like her quotes and writing and want to read more quotes
then u can catch her at instagram a_sheikh33

जब भी यह अखै तुम्हें देखते हैं
    अजीब सी बेताबी होती है दिल में
तेरे बिना रह भी लेते है और रहा भी नही जाता.....!!!
    यह अखै बार बार आप को देख नए की जिद करता हैं
अपनी सांसों में महकता पाया है तू जो हास दे तो पूरा दिन सवार
जाता है
    क्यू न करु तूझे इतना प्यार में,
तुझ को जब खुदा ने हमारे लिए बनाया है........!!!

A smile is contagious and in a good way. It's actually one of the very few things that you'd want to "catch" and then spread to others. The great things about making someone happy gives you a great relief at your heart ...   Being able to share and spread happiness is a beautiful gift that anyone can enjoy. Why not we start the sharing trend and spread happiness any way that we can? It's come back to you tenfold as well!

The next time you are out and about, try to do something special for at least one person and see how it makes you and them feel!
You never know ur simplest acts can create a chain of happiness that is contagious. So go out and be the light of the world n share happiness to evry one..

We have a long way to go, some tough issues ahead of us, and there will be some obstacles in the path ... But the good faith effort that's being put into this absolutely is encouraging to me and gives me hope.
But nvr be down by the problems u get on the way..
Remember you have to go long way from here..

Think positive....   Live in a postive way... It's hard but not impossible..

The sun brightens my face The moon shines my eyes And when I talk with you it lightens my heart

Debanjana Ghatak

Debanjana is an ordinary girl with big dreams in her heart. She is an ardent lover of animals, Literature, music, photography, Nature and a strong believer of God. She loves to dream and enjoy dwelling in her fairytale land. She enjoys the tiny rays of happiness hidden in the smallest moments of life. She calls herself a believer and a dreamer. Professionally she is an English and Soft Skills faculty and has a great rapport with all of her students. She has already worked on 150+ anthologies as one of the co-authors. Debanjana also has a solo book, 'Let's Sing a Love Song' published in 2017. In 2021 she has received The Fireboxx Award in Best Woman Writer category, an awardee of the Most Deserving Award in Best Writer category organized by AwardsArc, one of the Applause Awardees of 2021 and a Writer's Ink awardee organized by

Applause Awards in association with SillyFolks Productions, one of the Surpass awardees of **2021** presented by My Mini Tales in association with Inkquills Publishing House and an awardee of The Opus Talent Award presents by The Opus Coliseum. She regularly participates at various writing competitions and receives many awards for the same. She is also an active columnist of The Telegraph t2, Feedback page. She has even taken face to face interviews of well known celebrities along with The Telegraph t2 journalists. Debanjana believes in the philosophy of never giving up. She doesn't give up dreaming and believing in what she believes.

You've Painted Happiness

You are the rainbow in my
Colorless world. You painted
My woes into glories and praises.
You overshadowed my tears with
Bunch of laughter and joy. My life
Was occupied with despair and distress
Till you came, moved your wand and
Brought my lost smile back to me.
I was helpless and tears were my only
Mate till you played that euphonious
Melody which whisk my pain away.
Now I see colors all-around. You've
Painted happiness in my mundane
Soul. You've planted love in my heart
And unveiled the beauty of the world.
I take shower in the passion of your love.
I get drenched in the rain of your beauty
And purity. Thy countenance, thy smile,
Thy words make me shine like a star, a precious
And rare being which only sparkles for her king.

Synonym of Happiness is You

When my world was covered with
Darkness and I only could see hatred and
Feel fear. You came to me as a breathe
Of fresh air. You held my hand and kissed
My fear away. I was afraid to trust you
But you sang to me the song of victory and
Encouraged me to rise up and stand
Against iniquities. I listened, I breathed, I felt
Joy in my heart like never before. You have
Given me new life to smile, you have taught
Me to fly high and reach high up the sky.
You have made me happy and thrilled me
With every word you said. I am yours now
There is no one to fear because you are near.
Darling, you are my happiness and I find
Peace just by seeing your countenance.
You are the answer to my prayers. You
Are my moon shining in the sky of my
Lonely heart. You are my refuge, in you
I take shelter. With you I am free and happy.

I Feel You, My Soulmate

When the wind blows and the moon shines brighter,
I see your smiling face glow and twinkle like a star.
I feel happy and peace prevails around me.
When I hear the chord of my favorite music,
I feel you nearest and we are together forever.
This feeling makes me happy and I am in seventh heaven.
When I hear the loudest thunder and I am fearless
Because you are by my side and together we pray
As we feel its God's voice and we are safe and happy in His
arms.
When the first spring wind blows and I find you beside
Me. I am the happiest soul who wants to sing to the
Worlds and express her feelings that how much she loves and
cares.
When the first ray of sun touches the ground and illuminates
My soul with hope and truth, I feel happiness
And tranquility. I feel you, my soulmate.

You Are My Happiness

Happiness is
When I walk with you midst green wood holding each other's arms.
Happiness is
When you smile at me and I feel like a queen.
Happiness is
When you play my favorite music and we dance.
Happiness is
When you come in my dreams and fight for me like a chivalrous Knight.
Happiness is
When I find you next to me at the most needy hours.
Happiness is
When you stand by me and everyone says, 'No'.
Happiness is
When I smile and the reason is you.
Happiness is
When you appreciate me for every single achievement.
Happiness is
When I cry and I find you by my side to kiss my tears away.
Happiness is
When we get drenched in the shower of love and promised to be for each other.
Happiness is
When the coolest breeze walks through my window and I feel you nearest.
Happiness is
When I hear the rumbling sound of thunder and I know you are there for me to save.
Happiness is
When I listen to the soothing melody of Nightingale and I hear you sing a song of love.

Happiness is
When the monsters gathered together to attack me and you appear and help me to sleep.
Happiness is
When the raindrops touch the ground and I see you dancing in their rhythm.
Happiness is
When I smell the aroma of a freshly baked cake and find you are the chef.
Happiness is
When I am looked down upon by others but you are right there to console me.
Happiness is
When dinosaurs roared and I find you as a company beside me in the multiplex.
Happiness is
When the chivalrous Knight chases the enemies and your face resemblance him.
Happiness is
When I feel left out and sad, I see your smiling face assuring me that I'm not alone.
Happiness is
When I am afraid and hear your encouraging words that boost my spirit.
Happiness is
When the superheroes assemble against the supervillain and I find you standing midst them.
Happiness is
When I cry for my lost puppy and hear your soulful words
Happiness is
When I see a rainbow in the sky and it reminds me of your smile.
Happiness is
When the sun shines bright and you stand beside me to provide me a shade.

Happiness is
When the moon cools the night sky and tells me a tale about you.
Happiness is
When I dance to my heart's content and my heart gets connect to yours.
Happiness is
When I sing from my heart but not with my lips and still you can hear and praise.
Happiness is you,
My friend, without you my life would be meaningless and insane.
Happiness is you,
My lover, my savior, my beloved, I am madly in love with you and there is no shame.

Divya Baghel

Inspired by the title of this anthology "Khusiyon ki chaabi" Divya feel that Happiness simply means feeling good. It means the absence of negative and the presence of positive emotions. Her write-up 'secret to happiness' might bring a kind of positive smile in your face.

Secret To Happiness

Happiness is a masterpiece
resides in individual heart
It's something which can't find
It's a feeling to feel inside.

That feeling which we seek
does not depend on age
we truly hope it follows us,
as we turn another page.

Happiness is something
which sits next to us
but we look into
the future or past.

It's such a little word
sometime comes so easy
sometime seems absurd.

Happiness is the state of mind
nowhere else you can find
The secret to happiness is 'no secret'
just enjoy the moment and live the life.

Dr. B. Farheen khan

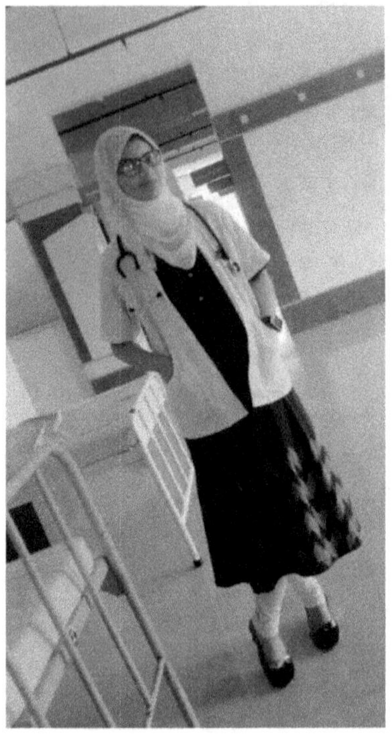

An eccentric girl who is a doctor by profession and writer by passion.

*She always had a mutual relationship with pens and pencils which made her interests in drawing and scribbling out of thoughts.

**Getting a life changing thoughts of millions is her calling

***She is usually a non-expressive girl to the world unless she is found surrounded with her cozy friend circle.

**Her friends would rather describe her as an easy going, optimistic and a waffle maker extrovert person.

You can follow her on Instagram @dr.farheen_khan.3

The Briny Deep Tale

Deep inside the ocean
Around thousand meters
She found herself encraved in between his arms
Finding difficulty to breathe
Yet enjoying the pleasure
Fighting for life
Yet blissful in soul
Entangled in his thoughts
Fighting for each second to survive
Yet she know she could not
Each wave striking harder with time
Finally lost their souls in eachothers thoughts with lapse of time......

The Second Bench (Part 1)

It was the first day of my school after a long vacation from states and all i know was nothing.....
Heart pounding faster
Legs shivering draster
I felt nervous but was confident to looks
Unaware of indian schools i arrived at the very end moment of the last english class wearing my lucky black and white crop top paired with black jeans with goggles uphead..
As i entered the class everyone started gazing at me and i was feeling like pooh from kkkg...
I was made to sit beside a girl named monica who was pale white wid silky hairs n elegant in her looks
She broke the ice first n asked
"hi! Where are you from???"
And i was quite for a moment understanding the question which was actually unexpected
I giggled n replied
" hello, im farheen from states"
And she exclaimed "woww muslim, im Christian, and she is hindu" pointing towards the girl next to her.
Class ended along with the chats
The next day as i was early to class got the chance to choose my place... And i sat on second bench as it was my lucky one always.
As she entered the class she insisted her friend to sit in second bench but to my luck it was only her who joined me.
As the classes started, our friendship grew deeper
We were more like sisters
Making top in exams
Sharing the foods to family
Benchmates to soulmates
We were just two with whole happiness.
There comes the summer vacation attacking our friendships

The Second Bench (Part 2.)

The quadrant gang

Summer vacations were hard to spend without meeting but our calls were never ending
As the summer ended we were an year older wid new uniforms, polished shoes and butterflies in stomach with increasing happiness to go back to school and friends.
A fresh new class with many new faces but as always my eyes searching only for her.
This time we choose the last bench as we were already spoiled.
As we continued to buzz around the school a bit more than couples our friendship grew older and our craziness for harry potter made a new entry, danisha who was sitting in front of us turned around as she exclamied "ohh harry potter! I just love ron".....we all giggled and were deeply involved in its stories.
The next days were weekly exams...
It was our chemistry text and was too busy writing and the time was up... As i hurried a voice interrupted me "hey no prbs its just a weekly exam, leave it... " and hearing it i just handed over the paper to her and walked out.
It was lunch break and a new girl, with brown short hair and sassy in appearance joined us with box of chips saying she was the one who just spoke to me at exam hall . She was manju, who just got transferred to our school added an essence to our friendship.
Our quadrant girls gang was all over popular in entire school
We started stealing papers to damping it in bathrooms
From a box of chips to sticks of icecandy
Exchanging papers during exams to scoring the same marks
We were living our childhood to the fullest but....

This school life period was no longer in time and the day arrived when we were to fall apart
The friendship was divided by subjects
Yet it remained same by souls
Our offline chats became more of online
Calls grew shorter as we were running out of time
But the thing that remained same was our love for eachother.
Now when i look back to the days im bounded full of memories in brain
Love in heart and
Tears in eyes......
I just wish we reconcile once again to laugh together

Tick Tock Tick Tock

Tick tock tick tock
The clock strikes again
But in no vain
I was back to room counting the 156 tiles
By Setting up the perfect piles
Talking to plants by Making flop plans
There were no friends But was surrounded by laughter
There was no TV but was always being entertained
There was no restaurants yet i had delicious meals
There was no college yet i had exams with openbooks ahead
There was always news of death, accident, exposures yet i was safe here
I wonder wats this life supposed to be
I thought of getting out of it yet i was loving it
A part time family became a full time society
I thought it could never end but it was just a lockdown to a front.
They called me crazy but deep inside everyone knows we were just hungry for society.

G B Akshaya

She is G. B. Akshaya addressed in the Township Villupuram her journey of life is to explore herself to this mysterious world . Her thoughts always stretches the mode of vivid vision towards positivity vanishing the negative ones. The way she was brought up into this writing world was that it's extracted from the containment of her heart and pens whatever her mind directs.

Though she is an 'amateur' her reaserch on the present time is on its own way. So she is locked up with her words authentically and soulfully

Gmail Id : kshjyothi@gmail.com

Happiness- A Candy

Time is the most important facet of happiness

Happiness doesn't need to be extended
When it just becomes a memory
It's retrieved.......

Feel your happiness
Because it might be countable

Age can pass over
But your heartfelt emotions
Can't be plucked rootless.

If u are a Joker
Be proud …
You create many smiles

We all will be awaiting for "THE HAPPIEST" moment
That magics on us..
Keeps us flexible.

Ecstatic Journey

Once in a time there was certain group of people who were just raising their voice for their own welfare at the Jhamnagar. The people had no option that they can be dependent on someone else. Those people living in a remote area it was like something bad that's going to happen and everything revolving around them was so weird…All over sides people were screaming like anything else. The village looked like it was dumped with bad tempered vibes.. Everyone were too panicked that .."What's going to happen the next"?

People had no religious belief . At the time of dusk all were frightened to go out their respective houses. Because of treacherous incidents moving around the place …..

"Dark skinned animals around the forest
In quest of prey , full of thirst and hunger
With sharp edges of teeth craving for peoples
Juicing their bloods" !!

Fields were in **Drought.** People didn't have much awareness of spiritual order. So the cause that occurred was too severe at Jhamnagar. The whole village had a situation of cursed one that all were diseased and some had injuries. The main course that they need to follow was to be forced towards Illegal things to get staged by those innocent ones… food and water accommodation were supplied in shortage of amount . People got sick and went down of their physical appearance.

"Face dangled of pale tone
Shaggy men ; torn clothes
In case a penny , people wandered
Here and there of need"

Imminently there aroused a temple at the view of a man named Shringar.He was somewhat in a perplexed state whether 'The power of god is really a truth one'? One day suddenly he woke from the bed and got initiated with his usuals..The fragrance of Thulasi plant near by made his heart fly away from the place. Everything that happened behind him was mysterious! There was no mark for his change only that was "Thulasi'.Nearby his house there was a sacred plant which was a matchable plant for God Vishnu .Besides the plant he sat for a while thinking of Lord Vishnu..,The minute every movement of him changed and he looked too studious about dedicating his whole life for his beloved Lord Vishnu

"Oh! My Almighty
Contented to have you in me
My words disappear only of you

You are the atom in me"

A temple with cobwebs around of forky thorns and unhealthy grass looking ugly . Seeing this Shringar thought of planning to rebuilt the temple and to furnish with some morally Idols. To carve the sculptures of the temple and to engrave the writings of some sanskrit mantras or sayings of ancestral precedor of Vaishnava . Days passed on, the committee members of the temple decided to have a festive for that temple.

On going of consecration every people in and around of Jhamnagar started to hault the plan by Shringar.Those really went in such a bad way that would gain them even harm.They all arrived to the temple so that Shringar was having a requisition towards the god. Within a few minutes all the people stepped into the temple. There was something that was a miracle to be presented there. The second when the villagers came a natural and good vibe extracted the negativity from the people ,that ruled them for those days. Consecrated works were moving on the other side without any obstacle. A priest entered in the temple with three Ashed lines in his forehead centred of kumkum.

" A plague once a time
Turned cure of divinity
Invisible but sensible
Your purity makes us feel dense"

Gradually the rate and announcements for temple to get renovated made its fame reach peak . Afterwards the people who pray of Lord Vishnu would be blessed with all health and wealth. Also auspicious days were given significant to the temple. Day by day people got an escape from the evil spirits . All in Jhamnagar were in a celebrative mode so that everyone stood tuned till the festival came to the end. People from the nearby villages were also allowed to worship Lord Vishnu and also to get his grace .

"Delightment was the only motive of those people

That they retrieved later
Of our saviour
Enriched us throughout"
When your happiness is traced!!
You and me
Like moon and star
Together with intimacy
Traced you in me
The time I was engrossed
With boat into happiness
Deeply sucked it…
The moment cherished me Atmost.

Grishma Ninave

A student of science and an admirer of arts.
A science graduate cherishing the art of writing, working as a project head at Flairs & Glairs Publication House. Published in the Editorial section of a national magazine as Aaj Ki Womaniyaa, in the first edition of 2021. She has won the Be The Change Award, AIBA Award, She Award, Applause Awards, etc.
A minion millenial with extra-large dreams.
Is in active rebellion with her mother about the number of books she must have in the house.

When not reading, can be found writing and reviewing books a lot.
Firm believer that music is what can revive and reconcile the world.

She's one of those people who love greys more than colours and she's like a colourful autumn too at the same time.
Admires old school love stories and retro music.
A Capricorn girl who believes hearts are more important than physical appearances.
Is into deep talks with a very few people, but believes they are the driving force of joy in her life.
Loves traveling to places where there are mountains, trees, hills and treks.
No wonder nature's beauty strikes a chord within her.
The guiding light in her life is the quote, "Don't search for happiness, because it's not something you find, it's something you create!"

Has participated in around 150 anthologies and compiled many titles too.

A Dream Trip

That will be my dream trip,
When I'll walk without fearing a slip.
With excitement I'll pack my bags,
And will crib a little when my cab lags.

Checking my essentials one last time,
I'll hear in my heart a chime.
Of the hills and the sky I will dream,
And everyone will see me with happiness beam.

As the train comes through,
My heart will turn cold like blue.
Holding my hand there will be my love,
Seems to be smiling at us, the sky above.

Reaching the destination makes our hearts race,
Enjoying there and sometimes making a face.
Making friends along the way,
To whom we'll have a lot to say.

We'll listen to the story of the clouds,
And wander shopping on streets with crowds.
The camera will capture what our eyes pry,
Coming back from there we know we'll cry.

To the memories made here we will cling,
It'll be a permanent affair not a fling.
Thinking of that trip we'll smile,
Wishing we could do it every once in a while.

And so will again sail our ship,
Wishing never to loosen our grip.
That will be my dream trip,
When I'll walk without fearing a slip.

Kohinur Ali Khan

मेरा नाम कोहिनूर अली खान है, और साहित्य में नाम रमजान अली खान है, मैं बानरघाट हिंदी सरकारी महाविद्यालय का छात्र हूं, मैं कविता,शायरी, कहानी लिखता हूं, और कभी कबार "तराने"भी लिख लेता हूं,   मैंने बहुत से यूट्यूब को कहानी भी दी है,और मुझे महाविद्यालय के तरफ से भी बेहतरीन कवि उसे नवाजा गया है

शायरी

एक मुकम्मल सा ख्वाब देख लिया कीजिए,
प्यार के नगमे कभी-कभी सुन लिया कीजीए,
मैं मोहब्बतों का दीवाना हूं बल्कि नफरतों का नहीं,
अब इस बात को मजाक से नहीं बल्कि शक्ति से लिया कीजिए !

शायरी

दो मोहब्बत करने वाले बार-बार झगड़ रहे हैं और उनके भी सुला
नहीं हो पा रहा लड़की गुस्से से लड़के के पास जाती है और लड़का
फरमाता है-
अर्ज किया है-

मेरा प्यार का कत्ल किस चीज से करने वाली हो,
अपनी निगाहों से मुझे मारने वाली हो, या
अपनी मीठी जुबान से मुझे मनाने वाली हो,
कहीं ऐसा तो नहीं अपने हुस्न से बेहकाने वाली हो,
जो भी हो यूह खामोश मत रहो मुझे एकतला करो,
चलो बताओ मेरा हश्र कैसे करने वाले हो !

शायरी

इतने झगड़े हमारे बीच होने के बाद,
ना जाने तुम इतनी सच सावरकर क्यों आयी हो,
मेरा दिल तोड़ने के बाद,
सच बताओ किसी और से दिल लगा कर आयी हो,

शायरी

मुझे नफरत, बगावत, रूठना, मनाना, चिढ़ाना-चिढ़ाना,   अनदेखा-करना,
शिकायत करना, जलना-जलाना, यह सब मुझे बिल्कुल नहीं आता,
आता है तो बस मुझे मोहब्बत करना आता है !

शायरी

खुदा और मोहब्बत के चक्कर में कुछ इस तरह लिपट गया हूं मैं,
नमाज़ी मैं पांच वक्त का था मगर अब तीन वक़्त का बनकर रह गया हूं मैं,

मेरी आंखों में नींद नहीं,
आखीर वजह कौन है ?

दिन में मेरे खलबली सी है,
आखिर वजह कौन है ?

बेचैनी सी गुजरती है दिन आज कल,
आखिर वजह कौन है ?

कुछ धुंधला सा मंजर हो रहा है,
सवाल आखिर वजह कौन है?

मेरे दिल में अब आग सी लगी है,
सवाल आखिर बजा कौन है ?

मेरा सवाल अब खुदा से है क्या मैं मरीज हूं ?
आखिर मेरा मरहम का इलाज कौन है !

Mahwash Ali

Mahwash Ali is a graduate in Botany honours with distinction in chemistry. She did her schooling from Loreto and grads from Shri shikshayatan college.She has been one of the topper of her school and college. Currently, She is working on her own book.

Contact her on- alizoya698@gmail.com

Mother's Happiness

A child takes nine months and stays in the womb,
It is the mother who takes care of the child so that the child
can groom.
She always protects her child from any dangerous fume,
So that the child is safe and secure in that particular room.

She is the most excited and eagerly wants her child to bloom,
She wants her child's life to be the most beautiful without any
gloom.
She has many expectations, many desires that keeps on
increasing very soon,
She is the one who prays for her child's good fate and a very
good fortune.

It is her unconditional love that never fades, never expires,
Her scintillating eyes in times of pain is something that gives
us hope, that inspires.
If something goes wrong with the child, She becomes furious,
she enquires,
These are some of the amazing qualities that everyone
admires.

It is the mother who is extremely patient in any adverse
situation,
Right from pregnancy till gestation.
A mother gives us the right education,
And shows us the path of aspiration and determination.

It is the mother who is very glad and excited,
She is a strong- headed woman, keeps everyone united.
Her HAPPINESS lies in every small little things,
So she remains enthusiastic and delighted.

It is our MOTHER who can bear the "UNBEARABLE PAIN
",
In order to give birth to the child who will be a genuine person
and very sane.
We must always respect our MOTHER for she is a blessing,
she is a boon,
For she is the one who makes us capable of every opportune.

Happiness

"The kingdom of heaven is within you; and whosoever shall know himself,shall find it". The individual who understands this will be able to attain anything in his/ her life. This proverb clearly delivers the message that any individual who can understand his/her innerself and can understand where his happiness lies, that too in a very discrete manner shall understand that the kingdom of heaven lies within us and that it is totally perception dependent. Sticking to the right path, helping the needy, finding peace and contentment in every little thing we do will actually take us to heaven.

In a world of stress, strain, rush and restlessness,peace of mind is of paramount importance. It is a state of inner calmness,serenity and tranquility, which brings forth happiness, tolerance, inner poise,inner balance and self control.

In an ideal situation, doing what one loves is the ultimate path to absolute Happiness.The fulfillment of personal goals and desires makes an individual happy.For different people, Happiness holds different connotations. For some, it implies a state of mind; for others, it might mean a standard of lifestyle. Not everyone has a similar point of interest from which they derive happiness. Happiness is directly linked with love and positivity. Thus, It becomes extremely vital for a person to lead a happy and a prosperous life.

The state of being happy mainly depends upon what a particular person wants from life.True happiness is never hostage to social acceptance or appreciation.

Heaven is regarded as the "highest place" , a paradise, in contrast to Hell. For me Heaven is more of a place where there is happiness, fulfillment of the heart, peace and contentment. If you actually analyse, Heaven is everywhere, it is just that we need to dig deeper in order to comprehend this on a much deeper level.For example-

1.Eradicating poverty to some extent by giving whatever little we can that can bring a smile on someone's face is not less than heaven.Helping the needy is not less than Heaven.The satisfaction and inner peace that we experience is to the power of infinity and is beyond words.

2.Relieving someone's sorrow is not less than Heaven. This is true happiness.

3.Saving someone's life, be it any species, is not less than Heaven.

4.The unconditional love received from our beloved, be it anyone, is not less than Heaven.Infact, we should reciprocate it in the same manner. This is true happiness.

5.Rather than celebrating lavish and opulent birthday parties, celebrate your birthday with the children living on the footpath who are deprived of everything. The children who long for such scrumptious cakes, delicious food, who have never tasted pizzas and burgers in their entire life.Celebrating with them is not less than Heaven as happiness lies in these little things.

If you involve yourself in social activities where you help the needy and provide support to the weaker section of the society, you can definitely experience happiness.Staying contended in life with what you have rather than Cribbing will lead you to happiness. By being thankful to God for all the good things that you have in your life will lead you to happiness. Having good people around you who can boost up positivity in your life will lead you to happiness.

Thus, I would conclude by saying that Happiness is everywhere, we all must have got a glance of it.Happiness is a state of mind which makes you feel accomplished in life.Happiness is an internal feeling, a healthy emotion that help us to stay fit both physically and mentally. Happiness helps in lowering stress and keeping away from any health issues. The reason of happiness may vary from one individual to another individual but You need to find out what actually makes you happy. So, if you really want real happiness in life then, you should understand that only you can make yourself happy.

Manjuladevi V.S

Manjuladevi Velusamy, born in a small village at Valliyaampudhur, karur. She completed her school education at P.A. Vidhya Bhavan higher secondary school, karur. She completed her under graduation in the field of Englsih Literature at Mangayarkarasi college of arts and sciences for women, Madurai. At present she is pursuing B.ed at Sri Aurobindo Mera College of education, Madurai. She had great passion on reading poems from her school days. To her,2020 Lockdown is the golden period in her life where she started to pen down her own writings and within six months she become Published Co - author for 20 anthologies and one of it selected in "Vajra world Record" and "OMG Book of Record".

Happiness - Unique Hidden Treasure

Happiness, a unique hidden treasure,
That cannot count and measure.
Happiness, a game that let our mind free,
And gives power to grow like tree.

Happiness is not about living perfect life,
Sometimes imperfect things in life helps to travel miles,
People wonder where it hides,
And forgets to enjoy their individual rides.

Life may not allow me to choose
What I need and dream , still
Iam wetting in the rain of Happiness
Where many people strive hard to steal.

Millionaire has everything except happiness,
Poor has nothing than happiness,
Happiness filled in everyone's heart, but
People fails to share and expand.

Happiness - Best Path To Lead Us In Peace

Happiness doesnot has limit on age,
But its duty to spread joy in different stage.
Each day it live within us, where
We fails to find, but making ourselves fuss.

Sitting near lover with a cup of coffee,
Looking each face and taking selfie,
Sharing true feelings slowly and smoothly,
The moment of wetting in happiness is like winning a golden
Trophy.

Instead of looking our past and
Dreaming our future in vast,
It's better to relax in a chair,
And to share happiness without Tear.

The intention of happiness is to spread positive vibes,
Because that is the best way to describe what we feel inside,
Though our heart scattered into different piece,
Happiness is the best guide that leads us in peace.

Happiness - Recalling School Memories

I still remember our canteen Tea table,
We give great shock when man brings exam time table,
We felt surprised when we won first prize,
Inspite of our friends Criticisms.

I still remember the way we act sad before principal room,
And we laugh mad on the way to classroom,
We forget to get our parents sign,
Our teachers consider it as a Crime.
We also pay fine for not standing in line,
Instead of crying we spread our Happiness.

I still remember how we forget our geomentry box,
And the way we eat with friends is the place of happiness.
The serious study on the way to exam hall and requesting
teachers to add Mark in answer paper is our hallmark,
where we felt happiness in recalling it.

I still remember the parents meet that organized just to
distribute our Answer sheet,
The way our teachers greet our parents where we expect only
beat from parents, the way we cover our notebooks with
brown sheet is our holiday worksheet..

Recalling our school memorise brings loads of Happiness
that melts our heart.

Is Life Needs Money Or Happiest Journey,?

Running in busy world just to live luxury,
But having no time to enjoy with lovable family,
Rolling with masters rule, making other to think fool.
From sunlight to moonlight working restless night,
Forgets to admire blooming flower in daytime,
And galaxy of glittering starts in nighttime,
But running in unknown path without Happiness in lifeline.

Every mighty minds beholds Office plan but forgets Spread
Happiness with friends and families,
Rooms filled with paper files than Vibes of Happiness,
Busy office meeting forget to share Happiness with their
kids.

Children cheeks wets in rolling tears than lovely kisses,
They longs for Happiness with their parents but,
Parents chase towards money than spreading Happiness with
their families,

Is life needs Money or Happiness ?

Meetu Chopra

मीतू चोपड़ा 25वर्षीय युवती हैं, जो की मध्य प्रदेश, जबलपुर से सम्बन्ध रखती हैं, इनको कुछ नया पढ़ने, लिखने का शौक हैं, ये अपने लिखन से कई प्रतियोगिता भी अपने नाम कर चुकी हैं, इनकी दो कविता तारे ज़मीन पर पत्रिका में भी छाप चुकी है। इनको कई उपाधियों से भी सम्मानित किया जा चुका हैं जैसे 'इंटरनेशनल कलम अवार्ड 2021में 'बेस्ट राइटर ऑफ़ डी ईयर' भी मिल चुका हैं, इनको ब्रावो इंटरनेशनल बुक ऑफ़ वर्ल्ड रिकार्ड्स द्वारा 'आउटस्टैंडिंग कंट्रीब्यूशन इन एंथोलॉजी' से भी सम्मान मिल चुका हैं।

गुल्लक

आहिस्ता-आहिस्ता खुशियों को संजोते जा,
धीरे -धीरे ही सही अपने गुल्लक में खुशियाँ भरते जा।

भीतर -भीतर इस ध्वनि के तूँ पहुँचता जा,
गुल्लक के जादू को थोड़ा तो समझते जा।

उछल रही वह गुल्लक खुशियाँ से भरी दिखाई देती हैं,
अंदर से हैं कठोर परन्तु ऊपर से नम्र,
वह गुल्लक बड़ी आकर्षत मालूम पढ़ती हैं।

गुल्लक की चाबी भी हमारे पास रहेगी,
जब ये गुल्लक के भीतर की खुशियो की बोली सुनाई देगी।

करिश्मा कर डाले ऐसी ये महान हैं,
बिना बोले ही बहुत कुछ कह देती ऐसी इसकी पहचान हैं।

उंमग से भर कर मन फूली नहीं समाती ये,
दुख के समय काम बड़ी आती ये।

साथी बन मुश्किल से बहार निकलती हैं,
गुल्लक की महिमा तो देखो हर मोड़ पर बड़ी काम आती हैं।

ख़ुशी हों या गम, अमीर हों या गरीब,
सबकी प्रिय बन जाती हैं,
गुल्लक ही हैं जो अपनी विशेषता खुद सुनाती हैं।

इस गुल्लक की महानता तो देखो,
बिना कहे ही सब समझ जाती हैं।

गुल्लक की अपनी ही अलग़ बोली हैं,
जिसको हम सब हैं जानते ऐसी ये सहेली हैं।

प्रिय बन करताप दिखाती ये,
अपने मालिक की सेविका बन चारों तरफ हड़कप मचा डालती ये।

मिट्टी से बनी गुल्लक तो हर किसी की प्रिय होती हैं,
कांच से बनी गुल्लक तो महाराजाओं की शोभा होती हैं।

 कार्य भी सामान हैं इनकी विशेषता भी सामान हैं,
फिर ना जाने क्यों इस बात से हम अनजान हैं।

गुल्लक के द्वार पर लिखा जैसे अनकही खुशियों का प्रचार हैं,
जिसकी महिमा को जान हम भी करते इसको नमस्कार हैं।

इस गुल्लक में ज़िन्दगी के अनेक रंग मिलाप हैं,
जिसकी विशेषता से हर कोई मनमोहित हैं।

महिमा में डूबा जैसे ये संसार हैं,
इस गुल्लक के ना जाने कितने ही अनसुने प्रलाप हैं।

खुशियाँ

हार कर बैठ जाते हैं क्यों आखिर,
ख़ुश रहने की वजह हज़ारों हैं।

निराशा के बाद खुशियाँ आयेंगी,
ख़ुश रहने की वजह हज़ारो हैं।

धैर्य और बुद्धि की हैं परीक्षा,
ख़ुश रहने की हर बार हैं इच्छा।

दुख के मोती भी गिर जायेंगे,
खुशियों के द्वार जब खुल जायेंगे।

समुंद्र भरे मन में सन्नाटा क्यों छाया हैं,
खुशियों से भरा बगीचा मेरे नज़दीक आया हैं।

खुशियाँ हर चीज़ में महसूस की जा सकती हैं,
ख़ुश रहने की वजह हज़ारों हों सकती हैं।

घर में माँ के हाथ का खाने हों चाहें पापा का दिया प्यार,
खुशियों की वजह हज़ारों होती हैं।

दोस्तों के साथ चाहें हों मस्ती,
चाहें हों घर में माँ के हसीं ठिठोली,
ख़ुश रहने की वजह हज़ारों हैं।

पिकनिक हों चाहें दोस्तो संग या हों चाहें,
माता -पिता संग, ख़ुश रहने की वजह हज़ारो होती हैं।

भैया के साथ हों चाहें कितना भी वाद -विवाद,
ख़ुश रहने की वजह हज़ारों होती हैं।

खुशियों में लिपटी प्यार और संयम की अद्भुत बोली हैं,
ख़ुश रहने की हज़ारों वजह होती हैं।

मुस्कुराती हुई माँ घर को खुशियों से भर डालती हैं,
ख़ुश रहने की वजह हज़ारो होती हैं..
ख़ुश रहने की वजह हज़ारो होती हैं।

खिलौने

एक पल इसके साथ हैं,
तो दूजे पल उसके,
इसपर ना किसी जाति का ज़ोर हैं,
ना किसी वाणी का शोर हैं,
ना किसी धर्म की बेड़ियां है,
खिलौने तो हैं सबके अनुकूल।

खुशियों में जैसे तार चाँद लगा देते,
बच्चों के हाथ में जब ये खिलौने आ जाते।

छोटे-छोटे खिलौने भी अपनी खूबसूरती बयां कर जाते हैं,
जब गुड़िया के हाथ में आकर ख़ुशी से झूम जाते हैं।

टेडी बेयर तो जैसे बच्चों का प्यारा दोस्त बन जाता है,
घर-घर में तभी तो सजाने के बड़े काम आता है।

खिलौनों से सजा घर भी बहुत अद्भुत रंग दिखाता है,
बच्चों के मन में जैसे मोर नाचने लग जाता है।

Monica Baradia

Monica Baradia is A
Student of T.Y.B.A English Literature of Sathaye College Mumbai.
She Aspires to be a Writer and her area of focus is Poetry. Poetry is an Art form that appeals to her greatly. She believes poem is an expression of Art and each one of us is an Artist. Penning down her thoughts is what she loves the most..
She Is well Know for her Poems and Articles in Support of Rights of Transgender Women and Also about various Social Issues of Society.
  She Has Decided to Dedicate her Work to her Mother Mrs. Vaishali B.Welis who has always been her Support and Someone who has always Guided her , Motivated her and has been Her Strength Right from the start it's all her Prays And Blessings all that she has Achieved In Life today.

Voice In My Head

It Follows me where ever I go.
About each other since ages we know.

Who needs An Enemy when You have one staying in Head.
It follows me everywhere , from morning till the time I go to bed .

These Thoughts are like the painkillers too much of it can be Harmful.
So better be Careful.

As it keeps Wandering here and there.
It makes me think I am in some Circus or some Fair.

Then I think when was the last Time it must have camly must have Sat .
As it keeps Thinking about This and That .

Be Kind To everyone You Have no Idea what is someone might be Going Through.
They Might Appear Happy from Out but something might be killing them Inside we might not even Have Clue.

Smile On My Face Fear In My Heart

I have Walked in through Darkness don't tell me about Light .
Sky looked beautiful even in the Moonless Night.

Don't try selling Dreams to those who have walked in through
Nightmares.
Everything has got washed out from in There.

Everything is temporary just sit calm and don't Stress.
Else your fear will overpower you in your Head and then it
will create a Mess.

If Life tries to break you don't Fear it is trying to make you
Unbreakable.
The day will no sooner come the Power over it will be
Unsustainable.

We all get in Life .
Let not fear get in to your Head or it will kill You Twice .

Smiles Hides Everything

Sometimes the Eyes can say more than the Mouth.
Sometimes the Heart can be heard shouting out Loud .

Sometimes there's an extreme Tallent in the Child who sits on the Last Bench.
Where as the one who sits on the first Bench might Just copy Teacher'ss Sentence.

Sometimes the Brain takes the right Decision then the Heart.
Sometimes our legs Know's when to walk away and be Smart.

Sometimes Pain is Necessary to rise in any Game.
If You like Peace ,Love and to left alone instead of being around People there is no Shame.

Sometimes You can actually hear someone's voice while reading their Messages.
Sometimes the mind actually brings the person back whose been lost in our memories since Ages.

I sat on the Chair and Thought to myself.
I was Just
Holding My Cup of tea and my eyes went on the Book which
was on Shelf.

I found my self lost Between The Pages of It.
As I kept Reading as if from it something I would Benefit.

I
closed the book and Sat There.
While I thought of this and that
my mind took me on a FAIR.

I kept Thinking .
 Keept looking
at roof top without Blinking.

Our heart is Just 350 Grams But
still it Holds So much of Emotions.
 Our Brain size is just 1198
Grams but still it Holds all The worries , Thoughts and
Tensions.

Nothing is permanent in this world not even our
Troubles.
 When You share Happiness with Other's even when
You are struggling with Your self Joy And peace Comes back
Double.

Share Happiness and Joy.
Forget your pain and
worries life is short live in the present and Enjoy.

Everyone Is Busy Discovering the World But Fail
To Discover themselves. Want to steal someone's Life and
Live and Excel.

There are some who Laugh out whole Day
but when they are left Alone they Weep .
 There are some who
Give Motivation speech not To Give Up on life they
themselves find it difficult to control their Thought so fail to
sleep.

There are Thousands of winds That Blow .
 We Might Know everything about the World but when we sit
In the Dark
about our own Self Nothing we know.

 Everyone Just wants to
Talk out Loud about Inventions.
But Fail To Talk about their
own Tenshion.

 There are people who watch out on "starts at
Night.
" There are some who with themselves silent Battles
they Fight.

 If You can share something ,Share Happiness.
If you Don't Belive me Try It And You Shall Witness.

Ms. Ishrat Jahan Noormohammed Khan

Ms Ishrat jahan khan is a passionate Teacher and a Writer she loves reading and writing. Loving and caring is her hobby. And keep learning and accept the positive suggestion is her quality.

She is working as asst H.M and project head

She belongs to North India and stays at Ulhasnagar (Maharashtra).

Loves humanity always.

Key To Happiness

My passion is a key
Which lead to me
Towards my happiness
And removes my loneliness

My passion is reason for smile
It develop my style
It improves my profile
So I am not fragile

My passion is to write
To make my life bright
And make life alright
And always be delight

Happiness is very precious
To get it it's very tedious
It's not easily grabbed
As it's always trapped...

अजीब दास्तान

ये है एक अजीब दास्तान
कुछ अलग सा है कारवां
कोई साथी नही मिलता
कभी कोई हमसे जलता

कठिन है तोड़ा रास्ता
लोग मतलब पे रखते वास्ता
गरीबी का उड़ता माजक
कोई समझता नही जज्बात

हसीन पल खो जाते
अपने पराये हो जाते
कोई साथ छोड़ जाते
कोई रास्ते बदल जाते

फिर भी ये दास्तान
चलती रहती है
लोग कितना भी दे तान
पर जिंदगी चलती रहती है

वजह तुम हो

जीने की वाजह तुम हो
मुस्कुराने की वजह तुम हो
हौसलो की वजह तुम हो
मेरी जिंदगी की वजह तुम हो

मैं रूठ जाऊ
मैं गुस्सा हो जाऊं
मैं दूर जाऊ
पर तुम्हे भूल न पाऊ

कई बार सोचती हूं
कई बार रोती हु
कई बार खोती हु
पर तुमसे दूर नही होती हूं

तुम मेरी जिंदगी का हिस्सा
है तुम ही हो
मेरी किताबे ही है
मेरे जीने की वजह

Family

Family is life
Without any strive
People always arrive
To give
you good vibes

Family is love
Which always move
Make you
smile
And make you important file

You are their part
Where
you won't be apart They are key to happiness And a medicine
to loneliness

Family is life
Without any strive
People always arrive
To give you good vibes

Neha Rahi

Neha Rahi brought up in delhi.
She is a typical delhite girl who is full of energy and positivity.
She is a nature lover . A lady with full of ambitions . She always try to find happiness in little things .

Hope you enjoy her amazing content .
Happy Reading

इश्क़...

इश्क़ राज़ी है
इश्क़ एक जीती हुई बाज़ी है
इश्क़ रंगीन है
इश्क़ बहुत हसीन है
इश्क़ एक मधुबन है
इश्क़ खुशियों का संगम है
इश्क़ इबादत है
इश्क़ दुख में भी राहत है
इश्क़ ही रब है
इश्क़ से ही ये जहां रौशन है
इश्क़ में अश्क भी है
इश्क़ में कई रंजिशे भी है
इश्क़ में दर्द भी है
इश्क़ तो मरहम भी है
इश्क़ एक पुराना गीत है
इश्क़ पनघट का नीर है
इश्क़ एक प्यारी नोक _झोंक है
इश्क़ दिलो की डोर है

ये ज़िंदगी..
फूल बिखरे है चारों तरफ़
पतझड़ के बाद जो फुहार पड़ी है
हर रंग को समेट कर बाहों में
ज़िंदगी खुद बेरंग खड़ी है
मैं घमंड करता चला जा रहा था खुदपे
देखा तो मैं ख़ाक भी वही हुआ
जहां से उठा मेरा ख़मीर था
सोने की छत भी काम ना आयी
जब आंखे बन्द हुई तो सिरहाना
लकड़ी का ही नसीब था
माना के मृत्यु जीवन का अंत है
लेकिन जीवन हर पल का संग है
कलियों को चुन लो कांटों से डरो नही
खुशनुमा रंगो को भरो जीवन में अंधकार से डरो नहीं ..

बिन मौसम बरसात सी हो तुम ..

बिन मौसम बरसात सी हो तुम ..
ओस की ठंडक तो कभी अंगीठी की धीमी आंच सी हो तुम ..
बेस्वाद से जीवन में रमज़ान सी हो तुम ..
खुदा का नूर तो कभी धूप में नीम सी छाव सी हो तुम ..
राहों में मंजिल की तलाश सी हो तुम ..
मानो तो सही मेरे पहले प्यार की शुरुआत सी हो तुम ..
नूर हो तुम हूर हो तुम जो भी हो
मेरा तो फितूर हो तुम ।।

चलो कहानी फिर लिखते है ।।

चलो कहानी को सिरे से
 शुरू करते है।
हम अपनी मुलाक़ात
उन दिनों से शुरू करते है ।
था ज़माना गलत
मगर तुम साथ होते थे ।
क्यों ना एक दूसरे के दर्दो
के फिर मरहम बनते है।
मैं रूठ भी जाऊं तो
तुम मना लिया करते थे ।
तुम रुक जाओ राहों में तो
हम तुम्हारी बाहें थाम लिया करते थे ।
चलो उन्ही राहों पे फिर मिलते है ।
अपनी कहानी फिर लिखते है।
तुम ज़रा नाराज़ हो जाना
तो मैं तुम्हे मना लूंगा।
तुम मेरी हीर तो मैं रांझे का खिताब लूंगा ।
चलो कहानी को सिरे से शुरू करते है
अपने इश्क़ में फिर रंग भरते है ।
चलो हम एक नई ग़ज़ल लिखते है ।
तुम पड़ो वो ग़ज़ल और हम बस तुम्हे तकते है ।

खुशियां..

कभी हंसने का मन करें
तो खुलकर मुस्कुरा लेना ।
ये जिंदगी है मेरे दोस्त
गर फूलों की चाहत हो
तो कांटों से भी रिश्ता बना लेना ।
मैं ये नही कहता की खुशियों से बैर रखो
मगर बुरे वक्त में भी थोड़ा धैर्य रखो
खुशियां बेशुमार है राहों में तू चुन ले अपनी बाहों में
तू रख हौसला ये वक्त भी टल जाएगा
तेरी खुशियों में तेरे संग तेरा खुदा भी मुस्कुराएगा।

Payal Purushottam Indani

Co- author Payal Indani is a heartborn girl with lots of love in her eyes.. Heartbroken by her loved one.. Still finds love in everyone.. She is happy with whatever she have and also desires to be a author of her own book very soon.. Love legal practices but firmly interested in reality of everything..

Happiness: A Key For Everything

Life.. A full of race and box of happiness.. People live it to the fullest when they achieve something and curse it when they loose it.. Happiness and success.. Becomes the major part of our life...

Some feel it in being alone, while some find it with people.. Some stay away from socializing, while some love being socialized.. The ultimate key to be happy is the desire to be happy.. Fame, money, power etc., all these are just steps towards someone's "so called" happiness.. Life comes up with various ups and downs.. But the true happiness is when we enjoy our ups to the fullest and face our downs with full fledged heart..

Attachments are the worst..

It always leave us alone, either with bad memories or with bad past..

Why do we easily get attached..

A slight change in their behavior, makes us feel miserable..

Why do we emotionally depend on the them so much..

It is very easy to get connected.. Then why it becomes hard for us to get separated..

The journey from strangers to priority shows us so many things.. That we couldn't stop ourselves to stay away from them..

How can a stranger be so close to us that we completely rely on them for our happiness..

How can someone be so important to us in such a short span of time..

The feeling called love.. Binds us in such a beautiful relationship.. That we couldn't resist to get separated..

Just want us to be together forever..

My life and love turned to be the worst and also the best..
We learn to leave without people and also with people.. It's
not easy to pour your heart out when it is broken..People play
with it and then go away..And this heart becomes a toy.. New
people come, they join it and again tear it apart..From all
such betrayals..The heart suffers a lot..Still it loves
everyone.. And within it, have a lovely hope.. Even I felt
this.. Once broken by a cheater, my heart was still being
loved by the one who had a ray of hope to join it.. He loved
me in every way he could.. And made me feel to be the
happiest person in the whole world...

The craziest start of our love.. The desperate ones.. You always wanted to be my side. And I always ran away from you.. Rather from your goggles.. You and your goggles were exact opposite.. You with a soft and sweet heart.. And your goggles were scary as ghost.. But the actual thing which made me fall for you.. Were your eyes.. Heartbroken and beautifully beating for me to be with you forever..We completed a year together.. But still I feel as if I know you from yours.. You gave me the thing which no one ever felt of giving.. People either fall in love or they fail in love.. But when it comes to us.. We neither fall.. Nor fail.. We just love.. Unconditionally.. Truly.. Deeply and madly for each other.. You are that spark in the darkness which gave me a hope to live again.. You are a miracle and true blessing in my life..

We completed a year successfully.. With lots of craziness.. Fights.. Arguments.. Misunderstandings.. But the thing which was constant between us was our love for each other.. We used to trust each other a lot.. Lot more than anything.. We were dedicated towards each other.. Just a sight of each other gave us a sigh of relief.. With all such tremendous excitement and joy and fights.. The only thing which I realized was - You are the only one whom I can call MINE.. Forever mine.. Thank you for being the beautiful soul and love of my life.. And yes.. I'm proud to say that you are the key for my happiness and the the source of my survival..

Prachi Mayuresh Kunkalienkar

Prachi Mayuresh Kunkalienkar is a writer by passion .She writes blogs and is an avid reader .She has written many poems and essays as well as letters to editors and won many accolades .She has also translated a Marathi book into English and also writes poems,quotes Marathi/ Hindi and short stories in English .She blogs regularly on instagram handle – https://www.instagram.com/bluebloodedmumbaikar_tales/ and believes she is a true Blue blooded Mumbaikar .She lives in Mumbai and in love with the city .Mumbai is her inspiration and teaching is her profession .She enjoys listening to music,reading,writing,appreciates and loves art and meditates and writes in her journal regularly .

You can reach out to her at -prachi.kunkalienkar@gmail.com Instagram: bluebloodedmumbaikar_tales .A teacher by profession,a writer by passion and an avid reader .She has been

writing poems,quotes and short stories since the age of 6 . She believes whether it is writing or living a happy life ,simplicity and love are essential for both .She has worked as a translator and also and writes in English , Hindi and Marathi.She also has experience in doing podcasts .She appreciates art (in any form) ,loves travelling,music,nature and food .She believes one needs to upgrade oneself and not only be the best version of themselves but also help others to be a better person , humanity is the best religion.. "Never stop learning" one can learn anything at any age ,if one is keen .

Happiness And Life

Happiness is just a state of mind .
We search for it in various things and people ,it's within us if you know where to find .
Life is always fair but not always very kind .
There are so many things we need to constantly remember and remind .

When we are kids all we know is to laugh ,be happy and smile.
Once we grow up ,we forget to be thankful and happy , treating life as if we are sent on an exile .
Life gives us a taste of everything ,just like it is very versatile.
But we don't learn our lessons and only think of the suffering all the while .

Being happy is also an art.
Just like everything else ,you never know until you start .
Once you learn it ,teach it to others ,its knowledge so you will impart .
Our lessons, purpose and tenure here is limited, so one day we will all depart .

But till the time you are here, live life to the fullest and live in the present .
Every moment wouldn't be perfect but how you live it matters,so be excellent .
Some people think about the past and some worry about the future, atleast you are a little different .

Story Of A Small Town Girl

Words of Wisdom for happiness

I am Khushi .I found my "Key to Happiness " ,(Meri Khushiyon Ki Chaabi) . I want to share this with all my readers too .My childhood was full of love and my teenage years were a struggle.They said I would be happy after I got married .I thought my happiness would depend upon my husband . Things didn't go as expected .They said I could be happy once I have a child .But I went through postpartum depression and forgot to love myself .I felt guilty and unloved at all times .Struggled through raising a child,managing my family and job .Tired of making others happy ,disappointed that things didn't work the way I wanted ,not happy at my workplace .I finally quit my job .I took up another one ,though not sure but it helped me get myself together again .I started loving my job and teaching the little kids and the kids loved me back .I was happy . I started learning new things , upgrading new skills ,started writing poems ,enjoyed coloring ,reading books .I realised all this made me happy .I started doing a lot of soul searching work and realised that there were so many things around me which needed the change and i can lead them .I started dreaming of being the change and started working towards my dreams and goals . I am now able to manage my family,my job,my dreams and passion and raise a child ,and guess what I am doing all this happily . So what was that thing that I did in a different way? Well I unlocked the block and found my key to happiness within .I realised happiness was not about only having a family and husband and kids but also about your dreams ,aspirations ,your parents and purpose .It's more about you ,if you are happy and doing things that keep you happy ,motivated and going . As a child there are certain things that you are drawn to ,something that

you love ,something that when you are doing ,you are living in that moment completely and enjoying what you are doing .without worrying about the past or the future , you are just there in that moment . That is your passion and that will lead you to your purpose .Your purpose will be the reason for your happiness .It's your key to the best things and the key to happiness too .So don't believe everything the world has to say .You have a whole world within you .You trust that and happiness will find its way to you and also through you people will be able to unlock their true potential ,know what they are and meant to be ,and you hand over to them the best gift ever "The Key to their happiness " (Khushiyon Ki Chaabi)

Hope ,Love And Smile

When I was sad and looked into the mirror ,it was my reality that I couldn't cope .
A serene smile appeared on the other side of the mirror and said "Wait ,don't give up ,keep praying and the best will come ,hold on to the hope ."
I looked at people having the best clothes ,food and having a gala time and celebration.
I felt when would my life be like this ,would it only get worse ,better ,while i looked at others in admiration .

I wished I could get the best of everything in life .
To be a rich,famous ,successful person and also someone's wife.
While I wasn't that beautiful or intelligent ,who would I marry ?
My parents didn't bother ,my brother unconcerned ,while my relatives felt sorry .

Suddenly one day things began to change .
Things which were once a distant dream ,were slowly coming within my range .
From the best life partner to a successful career and a lot of money
My days seemed lovelier and better ,sweeter than the sweetest honey .

Now every evening I sit in my balcony and the breeze blows on my face .
I realise every moment in life is temporary and a learning phase
Everything is momentary and doesn't seem to be forever .
Only hope ,smile and love in your heart will continue to live together .

Quotes On Happiness

"Happiness is being in the present and enjoying the moment ,here and now .The memories of the past will bring tears in your eyes now and the future will make you anxious now .Is it worth spending time and energy in things which are beyond reach .Make the most of today .Live in the present ."

"Happiness is within you and you are the only source of happiness ."

"When I searched for happiness in you , I realised I was sad because you didn't love me the way I loved you and I felt i was not worthy .When I learnt to love myself , I looked more beautiful ,felt better and you loved me better than ever .Self Love is the key to happiness ."

Pratik Premraj Bhala

He is Pratik Premraj Bhala, author of shabdo ka safarnama, award winning poetry book and he is co-author in more than 30 books and also has fan base of more than 9.5k followers on nojoto.His tagline is CREATING THE WORLD OF WORDS and he is writer, composer,singer and award winning poet.For contacting him email him on writespratik@gmail.com.

खुशी का महत्त्व

खुशी, क्या होती है खुशी? इस स्पर्धा के युग में तनाव के बीच आपके चेहरे पर जो मुस्कुराहट ला दे वह है खुशी. खुशी हर किसी के नसीब में नहीं होती है और खुशी को कभी पैसों से तोला या फिर खरीदा भी नहीं जा सकता. एक गरीब से गरीब इंसान भी बहुत खुश होता है लेकिन कभी-कभी खरबपति अमिर को खुशी नसीब नहीं होती है. खुश रहना यह अच्छे स्वास्थ्य के लिए बहुत ज्यादा जरूरी है. इस तनाव के युग में जहां पर आपको हर समय किसी ना किसी चीज का तनाव रहता है उस कारण से हमारे दैनंदिन जीवन में से आजकल खुशी विलुप्त सी हो गई है. अगर आपको सफलता पानी है तो सफलता पाने के लिए आपके दिमाग को तनाव से दूर रखना भी उतना ही जरूरी होता है और आपके दिमाग को तनाव से दूर रखता है आपका स्वभाव. अगर आप दैनंदिन जीवन में छोटी-छोटी चीजों से अनुभवों में खुशी ढूंढना शुरू कर दें तो आप के जीवन से सारी तकलीफें तनाव कम हो जाएंगे. हमेशा विचारवंत लोग यह कहते हैं कि अगर मन खुश तो जीवन खुश जो कि अटल सत्य है. अगर आपका मन खुश रहेगा तो अपने आप हर काम बिना तनाव के जल्दी पूर्ण हो जाएगा. आप खुश रहने से आपके स्वास्थ्य में भी वृद्धि होती है और दिमाग भी नये-नये ज्ञान को आत्मसात करने के लिए हमेशा आतुर रहता है. दुनिया में ऐसे बहुत से लोग हैं वह कितने भी अमीर हो लेकिन हमेशा अपने मन को तनाव से बांधे रखते हैं और अधिक पैसे कमाने की लालसा में दिन रात तनाव में रहते हैं. ऐसे लोग न खुद खुश रह पाते हैं न अपने परिवार को खुश रख पाते हैं, जिससे परिवारों में मतभेद भी होते हैं और किसी का भी स्वास्थ्य अच्छा नहीं होता है. लेकिन वही आप एक मध्यम आय वाले परिवार के इंसान को देखिए, वह भले ही कम कमाता हो लेकिन करोड़ों की ख़ुशी उसके मन और चेहरे पर झलकती है जिससे वह परिवार हमेशा आनंदित और प्रफुल्लित रहता है.

जो इंसान हमेशा आनंदित रहता है और छोटी छोटी चीजों में खुशी ढूंढता है ऐसे इंसान का चेहरा हमेशा तेजस्वी रहता है और इसकी आयु भी बढ़ती है. अगर आप रोज के काम का तनाव घर लेकर आते हैं और आपके चेहरे पर वहा झलकता है तो इसका प्रभाव आपके पूरे परिवार पर होता है. और वही अगर आप रोज काम को अपने कार्यस्थल पर ही छोड़ कर घर पर खुशी के साथ आते हैं तो आपके सारे परिवार में भी खुशी की लहर होती हैं. ख़ुशी क्यों जरुरी होती है क्योंकि ख़ुशी वह एकमात्र चाबी है जो आपको दुख के बवंडर से बाहर निकालकर आपको सुख की अनुभूति कराती हैं. खुशी वह चाबी है जिससे इंसान दरिद्रता को तक हरा देता है. खुशी किसी भी चीज से मिल सकती है. अगर आपअपनी पुरानी यादों को याद करें तो उससे आपको खुशी मिल सकती है, अपने दोस्त अपने भाई बहनों के साथ की गयी बातों से आपको ख़ुशी मिल सकती है. जो इंसान स्वार्थी होता है और लालच के अंधकार में सत्ता के मदहोश मैं रहता है वह ऊपर ऊपर तो खुश दिखता है लेकिन अंदर से खुश नहीं रहता है. कुछ लोग अपने चेहरे पर झूठ मुठ की खुशी दिखाते हैं तो कुछ दिल से खुश रहते हैं. यह सत्य है कि जो इंसान हमेशा खुश मिजाज रहता है ऐसे ही इंसान के साथ कोई भी रहना चाहता है. एक मां बाप के लिए सबसे बड़ी खुशी होती है जब वह पहली बार अपने बेटी या बेटे को अपनी गोद में देखता है, किसी अध्यापक के लिए तब खुशी मिलती है जब उसका विद्यार्थी अव्वल गुणों से उत्तीर्ण हो , किसी मजदूर को तब खुशी मिलती है जब वह पूरा दिन श्रम करने के बाद उसे उस श्रम का फल पैसो के रूप में मिलता है, एक किसान को तब खुशी मिलती है जब वह आपने फसल को पहली बार उगते हुए देखता है. एक डॉक्टर को तब सबसे ज्यादा खुशी होती है जब कोई मरीज उसे दुआएं देकर जाता है. खुशी का कोई मापदंड नहीं रहता है खुशी का कोई अंत नहीं क्योंकि खुशी अनंत है. आपके चेहरे पर भले ही खुशी झलकती ना हो लेकिन आपका मन हमेशा खुश रहना चाहिए. अगर आपका मन खुश है तो आप दुनिया की सबसे बड़ी से बड़ी कठिन से कठिन जंग भी आसानी से जीत सकते हैं.

मेरे जीवन में मैं सबसे ज्यादा खुश हुआ जब मेरी पहली किताब शब्दों का सफरनामा का विमोचन समारंभ था, क्योंकि मेरी कविताओं को अब एक किताब में समेटा गया था. वह मेरे जिंदगी का अभी तक का सबसे ज्यादा खुशी का मौका था. जब आप बहुत दुख में हो तो अपने भूतकाल में हुए सफलता के लम्हों को याद करो, आप जब सबसे ज्यादा खुश हुए थे उन लम्हों को याद करो तो कुछ हद तक आपका मौजूदा दुख कम हो जाएगा. खुशी हमें कोई खरीद कर नहीं देता है यहां हम मेहनत से कमाते हैं. खुशी की कोई भी परिभाषा नहीं लिख सकता क्योंकि खुशी अपने आप में सारी परिभाषाओं का निचोड़ है. मेरा मानना है अगर हमें भगवान ने इंसान बनाया है तो हमें सत्कर्म कर कर हमारे जीवन में हमें हमेशा खुश रहना चाहिए. खुशी सिर्फ इंसानों तक सीमित नहीं है क्योंकि खुशी हर सजीव को होती है. अगर आप आपका जीवन खुशी में बिताते हैं तो आपके मृत्यु के बाद भी आपकी यादों को याद करते लोग खुश होते रहेंगे, आपके छोटे छोटे चुटकुले को सरहाते रहेंगे. कोई छोटे बच्चे को खुशी तब मिलती है जब उसे कोई चॉकलेट या खिलौना दे दे

. किसी नौकरी पेशा इंसान को सबसे ज्यादा खुशी तब होती है जब उसकी तरक्की हो जाय. अगर आपके जीवन का सिद्धांत है हंसते रहो हंसाते रहो तो सच मानिए आपका जीवन एक आदर्श जीवन है. क्योंकि इस दुनिया का सबसे कठिन काम है दूसरों के चेहरे पर खुशी लाना. क्योंकि इंसान दुखी बहुत जल्दी हो जाता है लेकिन उसके चेहरे पर खुशी लाने वाला इंसान सचमुच में महान होता है. खुशी चंचल है वह कहीं एक जगह ठहरती नहीं है उसके रूप बदलते हैं यहां तक कि उसका समय भी बदलता है, जैसे खुशी कुछ समय के लिए आती है तो कभी खुशी बहुत बड़ी होती है.

सच मानिए एक ही सलाह दूंगा खुश रहे अपने परिवार को खुश रखे और छोटी-छोटी चीजों में खुशी ढूंढे तो आपका जीवन सबसे ज्यादा सरल सुलभ और तनाव मुक्त रहेगा.

Rabadiya Gopi D.

Student of Sardarkrushinagar Dantiwada Agriculture University, Gopi Rabadiya comes from Junagadh city of Gujarat.

She worked as a co-author for 20+ anthologies and working as Compiler and the EPC also.

She is passionate to Agriculture.

She is a national level player in various sports.

She is highly attentive towards her religious beliefs.

Most of her write ups are based on love and Nature's feel.

Her poems are based on the fantasy of her life...

She thinks that fantasy can create your life better and makes your world cheerful.

God's Vehemence

HELLLLO GUY'S … Hope you all are as cheerful as the nature. So guys like me how many of you are enjoying your corona vacation.? I know I sound bit weird by using enjoy the vacation. Trust me I don't mean that but I meant to be at home with your family.
I assure that someone like me is busy enjoying the nature.
Do you guys also come up with several questions seeing the delightful nature.
Yes in that case I doo…

I think the nature is the most loyal towards itself. He knows the best way to express his heart.. That too openly which we humans generally don't. According to my way of viewing nature I will show you it's various moods
We will start with the dim ones..

Example: When very angry…..
As we can get angry nd we have mood swings why can't nature? So according to me the nature is tremendously angry at…. let's take our own name. Think that nature is angry on us for just you say ignoring him, not giving him actual care etcc. You know what will it do. He will just completely open up and heat us.
Hope you understood, it's about summer the hot noons. No comfort. The hot air blowing is just irritating.
But at the same time it loves you so thinks a bit for you and gives you delicious mangoes…..
Some like me may not be excited by mangoes, for them it's about ice cream, Gola and specially that 'Pepsi stick '. Remember? It just changes our mood.

Example : When very cheerful and happy.
Yes bro! They also can be happy. As like when you see your crush and even more when he/she smiles at you. ! Then my God

you are on top of the earth. Now yess you are somewhat right it's WINTER

I see like it's just that much excited that it comes to embrace you and tell you that it's just wonderful being with you. Yesss now if we dance and bloom that's the icing on the cake. That cool breeze blowing through your hairs and yes to the live bird's it might be the remembrance of your loved one. Again you start feeling his or her presence by your side and that awesome atmosphere is the only witness of your unconditional love….

Example: When screaming and crying….Yes of course as we cry and sometimes scream loud the nature obviously can. Think of those words when mummy or dadi used to say "ohhhh,dear see how much you have cried ..see the rivers started flowing" ..and of course when someone cries we say see the Ganga Jamuna started flowing .So taking in count that i know you have understood what I mean ….yes it's MONSOON....the tremendous rain and the rivers flowing both sides.....and still the frustration is not out we hear the loud screaming of nature in the form of thunderstorm ….

When sometimes a person is too sensitive and emotional his emotions have no time ,just comes out at any time as like the uneven rain ….came a bit and went . Again as we like monsoon and rain but we don't like the mud and dirty surrounding same goes with nature tooo.as it likes us and loves us but if we do wrong to him obviously he will hate us.... Again here also it's great moment for cherishing your memories, enjoying the golden days spent together and that countless hours of talks with our beloved Yesss exactly reading this much I guarantee many of you just blushed remembering someone and the others just went to those days that were life to him/her.

Example: When you feel like dancing and blooming aloud........yes again feel their dance sometimes it's on the top. More perfectly imagine your height of happiness and joy when you come to know that the girl/boy you have crush upon also has

the hidden crush for you...See after just reading this much a huge smile comes to your face and your mood is just like you dance ,jump and shout aloud and finally you confess I LOVE YOU and you know you are going to hear the same ....You just jump to the whole world as tell him/her to be yours .....Now getting some hint or...Ok wait I'll tell you it's the SPRING

As you gain new energy with the same thought of being loved back the nature too gains that blossom with new beginning .The flower in the heart start to glow beautifully .The joy of new beginning has no bounds...you start feeling interested in everything and every single thing around you seems like you are in heaven .The lovebirds that are found chirping on the glowing flowers .....The day becomes longer and more cheerful...It tells us to forget all our depression and just gloom ....It's like ISHQBAZZI ka season......That "O Janna....."coming to your mind feeling his/her presence by your side and you too lost in each other's eyes .... Enjoy the best feeling growing within

Example: When there is a restart mood.....Last but not the least now your life had gone through many phase and you are now blank your don't get what to do and what not ....It's just a time for a fresh start, forgetting all your past and living with your present and for future .....Yes I am exactly talking about AUTUMN ....Even nature has those bad phase but then too he moves on every time with a great new restart...We too are a part to this system....it's time to leave all your bad memories back and start a fresh ....As the trees shed their leaves off you too shed your sorrows and plant a new happiness more perfectly .

So finally I want to tell you guy's that feel free to share your feelings with someone as it's designed..... Even the nature shares his every emotion but the difference is just in the vision.....Find that vision (person) who understands your emotions and feelings....Start blooming as a wonderful flower and keep the surrounding soothing .Enjoy the bliss you get ....

Sakshi Maheshwari

Sakshi Maheshwari is a high-spirited and fun loving person with a bubbly personality. She is currently studying in 12th standard in Amity international School. She has keen interests in dancing, travelling and social sciences .She is an active participant in MUNs and writing competitions. She is a trustworthy person..
She can be found on Instagram @_sakshi_maheshwari

Happiness From Travelling

.CAN'T.STOP.WON'T.STOP.MOVING.

Traveling is passionate. It is the coolest thing one can be a part of! Travelling is an obsession as well as an addiction. It's more like a agonize and yearning feeling. Traveling assures unforgettable experiences and adventure. Each trip you heighten more, and every time you come home you'll be compelled to want to go out again. The feeling of independence and getting strong with each trip is mesmerizing.

When you turn into a travel freak you have a lot of common things same as other Globetrotter. You're hardly at home from your trip and you already start planning your next trip. And as your next trip is always unfinished you are always bag-packed. You don't wish to settle. Keep moving is a thing in your blood. You are super thrilled to book your tickets, hotels and look out for restaurants and food. The only thing that depresses your mood is not traveling. You have different currencies in your wallet. You have friends in different parts of the world and you taste special drinks and foods from different nations. Also, Your wardrobe consists almost only of functional clothes. And your shoes are just the most beautiful collection of footwear. You mater the skill to sleep anywhere whether it be a bench or airports and you never feel jet-lagged. Tour bucket list is never-ending and your passport is one a lot of people wish to have, it has a stamp all over it. Being an Itinerant coming home is a different emotion cause you have traveled so much that the place you feel comfortable and sense of belongingness feels like home.

Traveling is fun, adventurous, memorable, passionate, pleasant, fancy, delightful, courageous, freshening, open-minded, crazy, beautiful, care-free, enjoying, comfortable, patient, experimenting, friendly, spontaneous, capable, natures and what not. Traveling is an intimate and affectionate thing.

~Wanderlust Sungazing.

Happiness Is Love

Love is in the air. I am in love with love. And I love seeing people falling in love. Wouldn't it be wonderful seeing an intense romantic love story that lasted forever? But what if such a desire for love becomes excessive in everyone? Could love become an addiction to us? This is what the world says- In love addiction, immature love, love that is uncertain, external, blind, and beyond anyone's control. Love must be differentiated from other conditions, such as borderline personality disorder; in these disorders, the pattern of behavior is not limited to romantic love. Love addiction also differs from psychotic disorders, sex addiction, and delusional disorder characterized by the assumption that another person is in love with the individual.

There is no stats on the criteria for love addiction, nor agreements or documentaries on what kind of disorder love addiction is.

For instance, love may be an impulse control disorder characterized by impulsivity.

Others believe love is a mood disorder. People with love addiction experience mood states similar to those who are falling in love quickly or are in the early stages of intense romantic love.

Another possibility is that love addiction belongs to the spectrum like people with obsessions, those with love addiction might experience repetitive thoughts except that their obsessions will be related to the person they love but do not have health or cleanliness concerns.

Love is an addiction and can be a behavioral addiction. Behavioral addictions do not require the consumption of any kind of substance, but they share other characteristics with substance addiction. Like a person in the early stages of drug use, people addicted to love might at first experience intense

pleasure and satisfaction. Then they become habitual of these experiences and increases signs of love seeking and many other requirements

After all, what I feel is that Love addiction is normal and people love to have such addiction and can be a wonderful experience with the right person that your heart chose. It's completely natural. Some people try to run away from it feeling that it might affect them and their actions towards their goals. But love is something that finds a way from within a person to come out. Love addiction makes people do even such things they have never thought of. It is unpredictable it can happen anytime anywhere and with anyone. It does not bother any other external factors. It's just heart to heart connection that comes from within. One always wishes to have a long-lasting epic love or a love story to narrate to the world increasing everyone's belief. It has no harm if controlled with maturity and sensibly but its love man it can make anyone mad and make some lose their senses just for one thing that is love. So just fall in love freely with anyone without a second thought. It's ok to make mistakes. It's ok to fall in love with the wrong people sometimes. Some mistakes get made but it is alright that's ok take it as a moral of the story and move ahead.

Happiness From Pet Dog

WHY BE A DRUG ADDICT WHEN YOU CAN BE A DOG ADDICT!!

Some genius once quoted "Addiction of anything kills us from within and only lead to sadness and despair". Surely, that person didn't have a dog as his best friend. Being around a dog would always make you feel loved and cared for in ways that can't be expressed in words. A dog lover would just melt like ice cream on a hot summer day, after having eye contact with a dog's big & mesmerizing eyes.

Dogs have been humans' best friends for thousands of years. Your life might be a road full of obstacles; friends who might prove to be double-faced people but dogs on the other hand are there for us through thick and thins. Whether we go out for six minutes six hours or even six months, they are always happy to see us. Some studies have also proven that people who have pet dogs live longer on average than a person who doesn't have a pet dog. They help in the mental therapy of a person and also in reducing anxiety, pain, and depression. The calming influence of dogs also lowers the risk of heart attack by resisting blood pressure to rise.

Apart from all the other benefits like protecting the house, motivating us to exercise, and all the health benefits, the unconditional love of a dog is the main reason why a person owns it and can only be felt by that very person. Dog's don't judge you on the basis of your caste, race, sex, religion. It doesn't care whether you are good or bad, rich or poor, successful or failure. They just need a little bit of love and attention and in return, they would fill your life with happiness and love. They appreciate everything we do for them.

It's somewhat true that having a dog in our life makes us better human beings. It is the only thing in this whole world that loves you more than it loves himself.

Happiness Is Books

It is often said that when you open a book, you open a new world. Being addicted to books is one of the best feelings in the world. One's attitude and personality change completely when they start reading books. They help in improving our imagination, memory, understanding, and knowledge. Books are just like human beings. They are countless in number, but a reader gets to know about a few of them only. They give us support in times of loneliness. They teach us everything we need to know about life. Most importantly, we can't judge how a book is from the inside on the basis of its physical appearance. We often hear in our childhood that books are our best friends and they indeed are. Unlike human beings, they don't expect anything from us and don't judge us. Also, they improve our standard of living. They inspire us, encourage us at times when we feel defeated. Indeed, a book is a gift that we can open again and again. There is no doubt that one can get addicted to book. Wherever there is just in the story. Our mind starts thinking in all the possible directions that what is going to happen next. If you are stressed out, novels might be the best medicine. Reading not only improves vocabulary but also increases intelligence. Reading on regular basis is not harmful but if your reading habit isolates you to the point where you lose a friendship, cut of from family and avoid social interaction then it's wrong. It is important to limit our reading behavior for some time.

Tejeshwar pandey

जन्म ९ नवम्बर १९८८ , मूलतः हम उत्तरप्रदेश जिला गोरखपुर से हु पिताजी गुजरात पुलिस में अफसर पद से सेवा निवृत हुवे और उन्हिकि बदौलत हमें सूरत जैसा शानदार शहर नसीब हुवा। हमारा जन्म एवं शिक्षा सूरत शहर में ही हुवा है और सूरत में हमारा कंप्यूटर सेल्स ~ सर्विसिस का बिज़नेस है हम तीन भाई है जो यह बिज़नेस सँभालते है। हमारी शादी २०१८ में हुई और अब लक्ष्मी समान एक प्यारी सी बिटिया भी है जिसका नाम वेदिका है। वैसे तो हम पढाई लिखाई में बेहद कमजोर थे पर ज़िन्दगी के कुछ हादसों ने हमें लिखना सीखा दिया। लिखने की प्रेरणा हमें हमारे पिताजी के द्वारा प्राप्त हुई। हम पिछले १० वर्ष से लिख रहे है। हमें लिखने की प्रेरणा परिस्तिथियों और भावनाओं से मिलती है। हम अभी तक सीख ही रहे है। लिखना हमें इसलिए पसंद है की लेखन से इंसान अपने आप से रूबरू होसकता है अपने भीतर की आवाज़ समझ सकता है। लिखने की प्रेरणा हमें हमारे जीवन के अच्छे बुरे लम्हो से एवं समाज में बनती बिगड़ती घटनाओं से मिलती है। यदि हमारी रचना को पढ़ कर किसी भी इंसान के दिल को सुकून मिलता है या उनके चेहरे पर खुशियों भरी मुस्कराहट लासकती है तो वह हमारे लेखन को सफल बनाता है। भीतर छिपी कोई छोटी सी उम्मीद ,अंधेरे-उजालों के द्वंद्व और अपने ही तरीके से उलझता-सुलझता इंसान यही है मेरे लिखने की प्रेरणा है।

Insta ID : @tejkush_always_happy

Facebook ID : @tejeshwar.pandey

खुशियों के लिए दौलत नहीं प्यार ज़रूरी है।

यारों यहाँ उम्र बीत जाती है दौलत कमाने में और यहाँ लोग हजारों ~ लाखों ~ करोड़ो खर्च कर देते है बेमतलब की रस्मों रिवाज़ों और दिखावे में।

ज़रूरी नहीं की रिश्तों में पैसे खर्च करने से ही ख़ुशियाँ आती है ज़रुरी नहीं दौलत से ही रिश्ते मजबूत होते है। अच्छे रिश्ते हमेशा परस्पर विश्वास से सच्चे दिल से सच्चाई से और ख़ुशियों से जुड़ते है न की बेवजह बेफ़िज़ूल दौलत के लुटाने से दिखावे से। समाज के सामने दुनिया के नज़रों में हम दिखावा करे या न करे उससे कोई फर्क नहीं पड़ता हम कैसे व्यवहार करते है कैसे रहते है कैसे रिश्ते निभाते है इससे हमें फर्क पड़ता है और फर्क पडना भी चाहिए क्यों की समाज क्या सोचता है दुनिया क्या सोचती है उससे कोई मतलब नहीं पर हम क्या सोचते है हमारे अपने क्या सोचते है इससे हमें फर्क पड़ना चाहिए। जीवन में हम किस राह पे चलते रहे है इससे हमें फर्क पड़ना चाहिए। यदि हम सही है और सच्चे दिल से हमारे रिश्तों को निभाते है हंसते मुस्कुराते हुए आगे बढ़ते है, तो हमें समाज या दुनिया क्या कहता है क्या सोचता है उसकी फ़िक्र नहीं करनी चाहिए क्यों की हम सही है और सही रास्तों पर है और हमारे रिश्ते विश्वाश की डोर से मज़बूती से जुड़े है तो हमें फिक्र करने की कोई जरुरत नहीं बस हमेशा हसते मुस्कुराते हुवे और खुशिया बांटते हुवे आगे बढ़ाते रहना चाहिए।

खुशियों के लिए दौलत ज़रूरी नहीं प्यार ज़रूरी है दिखावा ज़रूरी नहीं दिल का मिलना ज़रूरी है।

दर्द हमें भी होता है।

एक बच्चा चाहे वो लड़की हो या लड़का इनका रोने पर कोई काबू नहीं होता हैं. वो कभी भी रोने लगते है, लोग उनके बारें में क्या सोचेंगे ये परवाह किए बिना. क्योंकि उनमें इतनी समझ होती ही नहीं हैं. चाहे महिलाएं इमोशनली कितनी ही स्ट्रांग हो वो एक ना एक दिन अपने आप को रोने से रोक नहीं पाती हैं. लेकिन आदमी बहुत मुश्किल से आप को रोते हुए दिखेंगे ।

असली मर्द कभी रोते नहीं, क्योंकि उनमें से कई पुरुष आंसूओं को कमजोरी की निशानी मानते हैं। पुरुषों के हार्मोन भी उनके भावनात्मक अभिव्यक्तियों को रोकते हैं।

क्या पता की ये सच है की नहीं पर मेरा यह मनाना है और अब तक का अनुभव यह है की हम एक ऐसे समाज में रहते हैं जहां महिलाओं के पास ही रोने के सभी अधिकार हैं केवल वे ही खुशी या दुख के क्षणों में अपनी भावनाओं को रो कर व्यक्त कर सकती हैं। बचपन से ही हम पुरुषों को अपनी भावनाओं को दबाना सिखाया जाता हैं हमें ये बताया जाता है की मर्द लडके या पुरुष कभी रोते नहीं कभी भी हमें लोगों के सामने हमारे आंसुओ को व्यक्त नहीं करना चाहिए ।

हमारा यह मानना है की अक्सर पुरुष ना रोने की वजह से एक घातक उदासी अनुभव करते हैं। पुरुष सारे दर्द को अपने ही भीतर समेटे हुए खुद को बंद कर लेते है, जो कभी भी बाहर नहीं आने देता । हम सब में से बहुत से लोग इस दर्द को अपने सीने में ही दफना देते है और अन्ततः वे अपने ही जीवन का अंत कर लेते है। शायद औरतों की तुलना में पुरुष अधिक उदासीनता का सामना करते हैं, जिसका एक कारण ना रोना भी हो सकता है। हम पुरुषों को उनकी संवेदनशीलता, कष्ट, और भावुक्ता, कमजोरी दिखाने के लिए रोने की शायद हमारे मर्दो का समाज हमें अनुमति नहीं देता।

जीवनभर पुरुष अपने भीतर एक छबि लेकर चलते रहते है, जिस में उनको एक शक्तिशाली सुपर हीरो की तरह चित्रित किया गया है। लेकिन वास्तव में महिलाओं की तरह पुरुषों में भी भावनाएँ, संवेदनाएँ, दर्द और संवेदनशीलता होती हैं, जिन्हें वो भी व्यक्त करना

चाहते हैं। बचपन से हम पुरुषो को समाज ने ग़लत परिभाषा दी है। एक आदमी होने का मतलब एक लड़का होने का मतलब उन्हें हमेशा नियंत्रण में और प्रमुख रहना चाहिए। फिर पुरुषो के लिए अपनी भावनाओं को दिखाना कायरता की निशानी होती है। पुरुषो को कभी भी अपनी भावनाओं को व्यक्त नहीं करना चाहिए । पुरुषों के लिए रोने का मतलब, वे महिलाओं की तरह बर्ताव कर रहे हैं। भावुक और कमजोर दिल वाले है। सबसे बड़ी कठिनाई तो तब होती है जब दूसरे पुरुषों द्वारा ही ये कहा जाता हैं कि "मर्दों की तरह काम करो" मर्दों कभी रोते नहीं । इस बात का क्या अर्थ है ? क्या आदमी होने का अर्थ यह है कि वे अपनी भावनाएँ ना व्यक्त करें? क्या इसका अर्थ यह है कि हर समय पुरुष कठोर रहें ? पर ऐसा क्यो ? पूरी ज़िंदगी हम पुरुष मर्दानगी की ग़लत परिभाषा के साथ जीनें को बाध्य क्यों हैं।

हमारे तो यहाँ मानना है की जब आप कुछ महसूस करे तो खुद को व्यक्त करने के लिए ज़रूरत पड़ने पर रोएँ रोना जरुरी है। रोने से मन हलका होजाता है भीतर का भारीपन कुछ हल्का सा हो जाता है। पुरुषो को बिना कोई मुखौटा पहने अपनी भावनाओं को साफ़ साफ़ व्यक्त करना चाहिए। हमारे रोने से दूसरे लोग क्या सोचते है, उसकी चिंता नहीं करने चाहिए।

शायद सदियों से चली आ रही धारणा कि रोना औरतों की निशानी हैं कि वजह से आदमी रोने से बेहतर अपने ज़ज्बातों को छिपाना बेहतर समझते हों. लेकिन है तो वो भी इंसान ही कुछ मौके ऐसे होते हैं कि वो चाहकर भी अपना रोना नहीं रोक पाते हैं. और अपने आप को रोने से रोकना भी नहीं चाहिए और ये धारणा टूटनी चाहिए की हम लडके है या हम पुरुष है हम कभी रोते नहीं।

भीतर से ये बात निकल के आती है
हमारे रोने पर हसने वाले ए लोगो,
तुम्हे बस हमें समझने का एक बेहतर नज़रिया चाहिए।
हम भी बिल्कुल तुम्हारे जैसे होते हैं।
ये बात हमेशा याद रखना की लड़के भी रोते हैं ।।

आज लोग कितने खुश हैं ?

क्या लोग अतीत में सबसे ज्यादा खुश थे? विभिन्न समाजों के लोग अपने जीवन से कितने संतुष्ट हैं? और हमारे रहने की स्थिति इस सब को कैसे प्रभावित करती है?

उत्तर देने के लिए ये कठिन प्रश्न हैं; लेकिन वे ऐसे प्रश्न हैं जो निस्संदेह हम में से प्रत्येक के लिए व्यक्तिगत रूप से मायने रखते हैं। वास्तव में, आज, जीवन की संतुष्टि और खुशी सामाजिक विज्ञान में केंद्रीय अनुसंधान क्षेत्र हैं, जिसमें 'मुख्यधारा' का अर्थशास्त्र भी शामिल है।

सामाजिक वैज्ञानिक अक्सर सलाह देते हैं कि व्यक्तिपरक कल्याण के उपायों को आर्थिक समृद्धि के सामान्य उपायों को बढ़ाना चाहिए, जैसे कि जीडीपी प्रति व्यक्ति ।1 लेकिन खुशी को कैसे मापा जा सकता है? क्या समय और स्थान पर खुशी की विश्वसनीय तुलना है जो हमें इस बात का सुराग दे सकती है कि लोग खुद को 'खुश' घोषित करने के लिए क्या करते हैं?

इस प्रविष्टि में, हम उन डेटा और अनुभवजन्य साक्ष्यों पर चर्चा करते हैं जो इन सवालों के जवाब दे सकते हैं। यहां हमारा ध्यान स्व-रिपोर्ट की गई खुशी और जीवन की संतुष्टि के सर्वेक्षण-आधारित उपायों पर होगा। यहां डेटा का खुलासा करने का पूर्वावलोकन है।

जीवन की संतुष्टि और खुशी के बारे में लोगों से पूछते हुए सर्वेक्षण उचित सटीकता के साथ व्यक्तिपरक कल्याण को मापते हैं। जीवन की संतुष्टि और खुशी व्यापक रूप से दोनों देशों के भीतर और भिन्न होती है। यह केवल डेटा पर एक झलक लेता है यह देखने के लिए

कि लोगों को खुशी के स्तर के एक व्यापक स्पेक्ट्रम के साथ वितरित किया जाता है।

अमीर लोग कहते हैं कि वे गरीब लोगों की तुलना में अधिक खुश हैं; अमीर देशों में उच्च औसत खुशी का स्तर होता है; और समय के साथ, अधिकांश देशों ने निरंतर आर्थिक विकास का अनुभव किया है, उन्होंने खुशी के स्तर में वृद्धि देखी है। इसलिए सबूत बताते हैं कि आय और जीवन की संतुष्टि एक साथ चलते हैं। शादी या तलाक जैसी महत्वपूर्ण जीवन की घटनाएं हमारी खुशी को प्रभावित करती हैं, लेकिन आश्चर्यजनक रूप से लंबे समय तक प्रभाव रखती हैं। सबूत बताते हैं कि लोग परिवर्तनों के लिए अनुकूल होते हैं।

Zala Ramiben Devsibhai Sandeshi

Zala Ramiben A 33Year Old   writer. From Veraval ,Gir Somanath. Her workplace at Bharuch District.She Is a Writer and actor . She Loves To Write On Feelings And Emotions Of Human Kind. government job as teacher.. She Gets Inspired By The Shreemad Bhagavad Geeta and Sunita William.She is humble lover of Value educational drama.She got many awards in literature like Vajra world record certificate,book of india world record certificate and OMG world record certificate,also got many trophies,madals in literature.

प्रेक्टिकल

होंगे दुःखी मन से दुगना दुःख   पहोचायेगा जग ।
 उठायेंगे मजबूरी का फायदा इस
दुनिया के लोग।।
आए अगर रोना चार दीवारों के बीच रो लेना।
मगर शेर की तरह अपना दरवाजा खोलना।।
आंसुओ से भरी आंखों के साथ कीसी के सामने जाएगे ।
लगा कर सलाहों की वणजार मगज आपका घुमाएंगे।।
दर्द तुम्हारे जानेंगे रोते हुए।
पीछे से निंदा करेंगे हंसते हुए।।
अरज कर रही संदेशी झोली फैलाकर।
मिलेगा नमक हर घर,न मिले महरम कीसी घर।।
प्यार दो तो पागल माने ।
ना दो तो बुरा माने।।
वो ही टीक शके है इस दुनिया के सामने।
दिमाग चलाकर जो प्रेकटीकल रहना जाने।।
नहीं ये दुनिया उसकी ,जो जानता है रोना और दुःख सहना।
ये दुनिया है उसकी जो जानता है हक्क के लिए लड़ना।।

   शोर्ट एवं स्वीट
आंखें खोलने का एकमात्र साधन
मुसीबत ही मुसीबत।। धबराओ मत।।

धर्म और मूल्योका महत्व

धर्मका और मूल्योका महत्व हमारे जीवन मे धर्मका और मूल्योका बहोत महत्व है।धर्म हमे जीना शीखाते है।आज किसीको भी बोलो धार्मिक पुस्तक पढ़ने कहते है ये विज्ञान का युग है। एकवीसवीं सदीमे विज्ञानकी बाते अच्छी लगती है ,धर्मकी नही।वो लोग कयू भूल जाते है की रामायण और महाभारत ये हमारे कुटुम्ब की ही कहानी है।आज के समय में भी कइ मंथरा है जो कुटुंब क्लेश करवाती है। उससे बचना रामायण शीखाती है। आज कई स्त्री छोटी छोटी बातों में अपना घर छोड़ के चली जाती है।उनको सीता से सीखना चाहिए।आज यहां रावण भी है उससे बचना है तो मर्यादा में रहना पसंद करो।   महाभारत शीखाता है कीसीका अपमान मत करो। अपमान मृत्यु समान है।अपने हक्क के लिए लड़ना चाहिए।   गीता शीखाती है ये जीवन रो कर बेठने के लिए नहीं बल्कि हिम्मत से लडने के लिए है। आए दिन आत्महत्या के किस्से सुनाते हैं इस परिस्थिति में गीता के ज्ञान से ही प्रेरणा मीलती है। जब सत्य की बात आती है तो कहते हैं कि यह तो कलयुग है लेकिन उनके सामने अगर कोई झूठ बोले तो कहते हैं मुझे झूठ से सख्त नफरत है नफरत है।जब प्यार की बातें करते हैं तो कहेंगे कलियुग में सच्चा प्यार नहीं होता मगर खूद को सच्चे प्यार की आवश्यकता है।

अधुरा स्वप्न

आज अंजना बहुत ही खुश हैं। भारत सरकार के द्वारा दो दिन के बाद मुझे श्रेष्ठ लेखिका का अवार्ड मिलने वाला है। मुझे दुनिया की सारी खुशी मिलेगी।

"बस अंजू अब तो तुम दिल्ली जाने के लिए पैकिंग शुरू कर दे ,हम दोनों जाएंगे, कुदरत सब लोगों के सारे सपने साकार नहीं करती है। हमारे आंगन में छोटे बच्चे की किलकारी सुनने का स्वप्न साकार नहीं हुआ तो क्या हुआ यह स्वप्न तो साकार हुआ।

अंजना भी मिश्रित अनुभूति कर रही है ।सुबह से पैकिंग कार्य में व्यस्त थकी हारी अंजना को चक्कर आने लगे। डॉक्टर आकर बोले थोड़े टेस्ट करवाने पड़ेंगे। दूसरे ही दिन उन्होंने अपनी फ्रेंड को फोन जोडकर बोली, तुम मेरा सन्मान और राशि को स्वीकार कर लेना मेरे दिल की नजदीक रहने वाला स्वप्न साकार होने जा रहा है।।

दर्पण

इस समाज में सभीको सौंदर्य पसंद है, बाहरी दिखावे पसंद है, मैं तो बदसुरत हूं, में तो इतनी अच्छी दिखती भी नहीं हु। कोई मुझसे बात भी नहीं करता है। अब तो मुझे अपने आप से नफरत होने लगी हैं ऐसा सोचकर नियति ने दर्पण से अपनी नजर हटा ली। मेरे आंतरिक आदर्श,मेरा प्यार, मेरी कलाओं का मेरी अनुभूति का कोई मूल्य ही नहीं है? ऐसे ही मनोमंथन करते करते अंत में विद्रोही बनकर अपनी अच्छाइयों को खत्म करने का इरादा मक्कम कर रही थी तभी मोबाइल में घंटी बजती है, नियतिजी आपको कल श्रेष्ठ शिक्षिका का पुरस्कार दिया जाएगा। और नियति के चेहरे पर विजय स्मित चमकने लगा।।

हुनर

हुन्नर कृष्णा दीदी हाथमे चोली और ब्लाउज़ लेकर ...कंचन बा के घर गए ।कंचनबा यह मुझे जरा ठीक कर दो ना, मुझे शाम को प्रोग्राम में पहनना हे। जी नहीं! मुझे नवरात्री के बहोत सारे काम हे मुझे साँस लेने तक की फुरसद नहीं हे। फटाक से मना कर दिया। छह छह दिंनो से धक्के खाने वाली पढी लिखी वर्किंग वुमन को देखकर पडोशी सुमनबहन से रहा न गया और वो बोल पडी मेरी बेटी को तो विद्यालय में सिलाई गुनाई सब कुछ शिखाया जाता हे कल किसीभी प्रकार की लाचारी का सामना न करना पड़े कृष्णा दीदी स्वगत बोले काश हमारे ज़माने में भी ऐसा शिक्षण होता। फटे हुए ब्लाउज़ में पड़े छेद के बिच से सिलाई करते हुए कंचन बा को देखते ही रहे

Flairs and Glairs, a platform by a student for the students. We are esteemed youth struggling to carve out our path for our future and we follow a basic mindset Since everyone is not born with all-round skills. Joining hands with people who are born to execute it with perfection is the best way to evolve. Self-Evolution is the need of the hour but, evolving as a community is what we strive for. The initiative as kickstarted by, Founder- Mr. Shubham Shah with the motive to utilize the skillset and talent of writing has now a team of 10+ people who are actively participating into newer forms of learning and discovering talents among youngsters. We Provide platform and services like Publishing opportunities, Open mics, Workshops, Hands-on training. Operating with Brand Name of Flairs and Glairs (Publication House), we offer the chance of elevating a passionate writer to an esteemed author With Brand name Teekhe Zasbaaat. We bring to you an opportunity to get accustomed with the Public Speaking and Presenting of Thoughts along with regular challenges to brush up your inking spirit. The newest initiative to extend our services we introduced in a new writing Platform- The Glittering Fables and Ink Over Tears.

We Choose to Fly Like A Falcon than to be

a Leg Pulling Crab.

To Know More: Infoline – 7781900870
Mail Us At-
flairsandglairs@gmail.com / info@flairsandglairs.in
Or Visit is at
www.flairsandglairs.com / www.flairsandglairs.in
Social Handles- @flairsandglairs @teekhezasbaaat